HOW TO *NOT* MELT A SNOWFLAKE

by John Swift

HOW TO *NOT* MELT A SNOWFLAKE

by John Swift

How to Not Melt A Snowflake by John Swift

ISBN 978-0-692-11595-4

Published by Winedot Publishing

Quantity discounts are available by emailing the publisher at winedotpublishing@gmail.com

FOREWORD

Times are tough for civil discourse. It seems everywhere you look, someone is offended by someone. You know how it is: if someone is offended by it then that means everyone ought to be offended by it which means no one gets to talk about anything.

In the old days, in polite company you were advised to stick to sports and the weather and avoid politics and religion. In these glorious new days, even the sports and weather have been politicized. So, you don't even get that! If you want to still have a conversation with people without triggering a meltdown, what can you do?

It isn't as if you can avoid the dilemma. For one thing, the biggest culprits, the so-called 'Millennials,' are going to be around for a long time. Theoretically, we're going to have to talk with them. Theoretically, they want to talk to us. Granted, the rest of us are only allowed to say the thing that they have pre-approved, but still.

That's why I decided I needed to compile this list of topics that wouldn't melt a snowflake. Having taken the measure of society as it currently stands, with an honest assessment of the Academy, mindful of the media, and scrutinized the conduct of the Millennials, I have documented for you all the topics that you can still talk about—without being called a bigot, fascist, homophobe, etc., etc., etc.

I hope the reader enjoys this list as much as I enjoyed assembling it for him. Or her. Or zin. Or... Lordie, never mind. You know what I mean!

Sincerely,
John Swift

THE BIG LIST

Without further ado, here is your list of safe topics: